D0331898

POWER
SPY RECRUIT

Zac's Skate Break
published in 2014 by
Hardie Grant Egmont
Ground Floor, Building 1, 658 Church Street
Richmond, Victoria 3121, Australia
www.hardiegrantegmont.com.au

A CiP record for this title is available from the National Library of Australia.

Illustrations by Tomomi Sarafov
Design by Stephanie Spartels

1 3 5 7 9 10 8 6 4 2

Printed in Australia by Griffin Press, an Accredited ISO AS/NZS 14001:2004 Environmental Management System printer.

The paper this book is printed on is certified against the Forest Stewardship Council® Standards. Griffin Press holds FSC chain of custody certification SGS-COC-005088. FSC promotes environmentally responsible, socially beneficial and economically viable management of the world's forests..

ZAC'S SKATE BREAK

BY H.I. LARRY

ILLUSTRATIONS BY TOMOMI SARAFOV

hardie grant EGMONT

Zac Power was at the shops. His dad was buying him new school shorts. It was the last day of the holidays.

Zac was 12 years old.

He was a spy. Zac worked for GIB. His family worked for GIB, too. GIB was a good spy group.

All GIB spies had code names. Zac's was Agent Rock Star. His dad's was Agent Tool Belt. His mum's was Agent Bum Smack.

Zac's brother Leon was in charge of the GIB Test Labs.

His code name was Agent Tech Head.

Zac was GIB's test driver.

And sometimes he had to stop the evil spy group BIG.

There was a long line at the school shop.

Zac was grumpy. 'Can't I just wear my old shorts, Dad?' asked Zac. 'I could be on my skateboard right now.'

'You can ride it later,' said his dad.

The shop lady gave Zac some shorts. Zac went to try them on.

'Dad,' he called. 'They're too tight.'

'Just do the belt up, Zac,' said his dad.

Zac grabbed the belt. The belt buckle had letters on it.

GIB

This could mean some cool test driving, thought Zac.

'The shop lady is Agent Cool Stuff,' said Zac's dad. 'She fits out spies with the best gear.'

'Hello, Agent Rock Star,' she said. 'These shorts were made just for you.'

'But they're too tight,' said Zac. 'They look gross!'

'And they have huge back pockets,' Zac added.

'Don't worry, Zac,' said his dad. He pushed on the GIB belt buckle. Zac's shorts made a loud fart sound.

Zac laughed. Then two small jets came out from the back pockets.

Zac heard a noise. He looked up. The shop roof slid open.

Zac's shorts made another fart sound. Then he shot through the roof like a rocket.

The jets stopped just as Zac flew over the car park.

Uh-oh, thought Zac.

I'm going to land on that van

with the big sun-roof.

Zac got ready to crash-land.

CHAPTER 2

Zac was just a metre from the sun-roof when it slid open. He went straight through the roof. Zac landed on a huge cushion.

'Hello, Zac,' said Leon.

'Welcome to the mobile GIB Test Labs.'

'Thanks,' said Zac.

'Sorry about the shorts,' said Leon. 'They had to be tight to stay on.'

'Those pocket jetpacks are powerful,' said Zac.

Leon went to a shelf on the wall of the van. There was lots of cool spy gear on it.

Zac could see space suits and loads of gadgets.

Leon grabbed a pair of jeans and a top.

'Put these on, Zac,' said Leon. 'I need you to test drive them.'

'What do they do?' asked Zac.

'These clothes have Balance Boosters,' said Leon.

'Balance what?' asked Zac.

'Balance Boosters,' said Leon again. 'They stop you from falling over and give you super strength.'

'Really? Cool!' said Zac and he pulled them on.

The elbows and the knees had built-in pads. They were just like skateboard elbow and knee pads.

'I'm going to turn on the boosters, Zac,' said Leon.

He hit a button.

The clothes zapped.

'That's cool,' said Zac.

Then Leon gave Zac a cool blue helmet and the most awesome skateboard he'd ever seen.

The skateboard had purple wheels and rocket jets.
The jets looked like flames.

'This Supersonic Skateboard can go 250 kilometres an hour,' said Leon.

'Sweet!' said Zac.

'Jump down hard on the board to start and stop,' said Leon.

Just then Zac's SpyPad beeped.

Every GIB spy had a Spy Pad. It was a hand-held computer and a phone.

Zac loved his SpyPad.

He used it to play games and watch cool movies.

'It's a mission,' said Zac.

BIG has sealed the gate at the giant skate bowl.

Agent Bum Smack is stuck inside the bowl and must be rescued.

Test Drive the Balance Boosters and Supersonic Skateboard.

'Uh-oh, Mum's in trouble,' said Zac.

'You'd better hurry,' said Leon.

Zac stepped onto the skateboard. Leon pushed a button on the van wall. The back door of the van rolled up like a garage door.

'Make sure you do your test drive report, Zac,' said Leon.

Zac groaned. He loved test driving. But he hated writing about it.

Zac jumped down hard on his skateboard.

The rocket jets started. Zac shot out of the van.

Zac knew exactly where to go.

He was out of the car park in no time. *This skateboard is so fast*, he thought.

Zac was only three blocks away from the skate bowl.

The road had a lot of speed bumps.

These bumps will be fun, thought Zac. He sped over the first bump.

Zac landed easily back on the road.

When Zac hit the next bump the board lifted into the air.

Zac thought he would fall off. Again he landed easily. *These Balance Boosters are awesome*, he thought. Zac sped over all the bumps.

When he reached the bowl he looked around.

It was huge! He tried to open the gate. But it was shut tight.

I'll have to jump over the fence, thought Zac. The fence was high.

Zac put the skateboard under his arm. Then he took a running jump.
I hope the super strength Balance Boosters still work.

Zac landed up on the top of the skate bowl.

He pulled himself up easily. *I love this super strength!* he thought.

Zac looked down. There were kids skating around in circles. They all looked dizzy.

There was nowhere to go because BIG had sealed the gate shut.

Zac could see his mum,
Agent Bum Smack,
skating around the bowl.
Someone was chasing her.

It was Britney, one of the
evil BIG twins. A pink
chopper was hovering in the
air above the bowl. A rope
ladder hung down from it.

I have to stop the BIG twins,
thought Zac.

Zac headed straight across the bowl at top speed. *I'll catch her as she goes around*, he thought. But Zac was too fast. He missed her.

I can't go slowly enough, thought Zac.

He did a 360 on the top of the bowl and came back down.

'You can't catch me,' called Britney.

Zac missed her again. He did the fastest 360 ever. Then he stopped.

Zac waited as Britney went round. I'll get her this time, Zac thought.

Just then Zac's SpyPad went off. It was a message from Leon.

Skate straight at Britney and do a 180 sudden stop.

Perfect, thought Zac. I can do that easily.

Zac skated along the side of the bowl.

The board was going at top speed.

Britney looked scared.

Agent Bum Smack guessed Zac's plan. She skated to the side of the bowl.

Zac did a 180 and stopped right in front of Britney.

But Britney was moving too fast.

CRASH!!

She crashed into Zac and they both fell over.

Britney landed in the middle of the bowl. And she was right under the ladder that hung from the chopper.

Britney grabbed onto the ladder.

'Take me up, Pinky,' Britney called to her evil twin. Pinky was in the chopper.

Zac got off his board and ran over. He grabbed onto the ladder just in time.

'Get off!' yelled Britney. She shook the ladder hard.

But Zac had his Balance Boosters on and was too strong.

'Cut the ladder,' yelled Pinkie from the chopper.

Britney climbed into the helicopter and cut the ladder.

Zac fell and landed on his knees next to his mum.

'See you later,' laughed Britney. The chopper flew off into the air.

'They got away,' said Zac.

'Don't feel bad, Zac,' said Zac's mum. 'You stopped them from catching me. And my GIB skateboard.'

'Do you have the latest one, too?' asked Zac.

'It's not like yours, Zac,' said his mum. 'Yours is the only supersonic one.'

'What are you doing here?' asked Zac.

'I was on a mission to try to stop BIG,' said his mum.

'But it was a trap?' asked Zac.

'Did BIG just want to catch you?'

'Not me,' said his mum. 'The skateboard. BIG found out that Leon was making a supersonic board. They thought mine was it!' Zac's mum yawned. 'Let's go home now, Zac. I'm tired.'

Zac and his mum skated to the fence.

Zac picked up his mum. It was easy with the Balance Boosters on.

'Get ready, Mum,' he said. 'We're going to jump.'

Zac landed on his feet.

'That's amazing,' said his mum. 'Your brother makes excellent gadgets!'

Zac took his SpyPad out and sent a message to Leon.

Agent Bum Smack safe.

Big twins escaped.

Send agents to unseal the gate so the kids can get out.

Zac's SpyPad beeped with Leon's answer.

Return to Test Labs now.

Please file test drive report.

Oh well, thought Zac. *At least I get to ride the cool skateboard back to the labs.*

HAVE YOU READ THEM ALL?

WWW.ZACPOWER.COM

TEST DRIVE REPORT

Balance Boosters

★★★★★

These clothes were awesome. You could never ride the Supersonic without them. You'd just crash and burn. Can I keep them?

GIB Supersonic Skateboard

This skateboard is super cool and it looks awesome. But it needs speed control!